The Orchard Book of
NURSERY STORIES

Sophie Windham

ORCHARD BOOKS

For Bruce and Lily

ORCHARD BOOKS
96 Leonard Street, London EC2A 4RH
Orchard Books Australia
14 Mars Road, Lane Cove, NSW 2066
ISBN 1 85213 189 6 (hardback)
ISBN 1 85213 503 4 (paperback)
First published in Great Britain 1991
First paperback publication 1993
Text copyright © Orchard Books 1991
Illustrations copyright © Sophie Windham 1991
A CIP catalogue record for this book is available from the British Library.
Printed in Singapore

The Orchard Book of
NURSERY STORIES

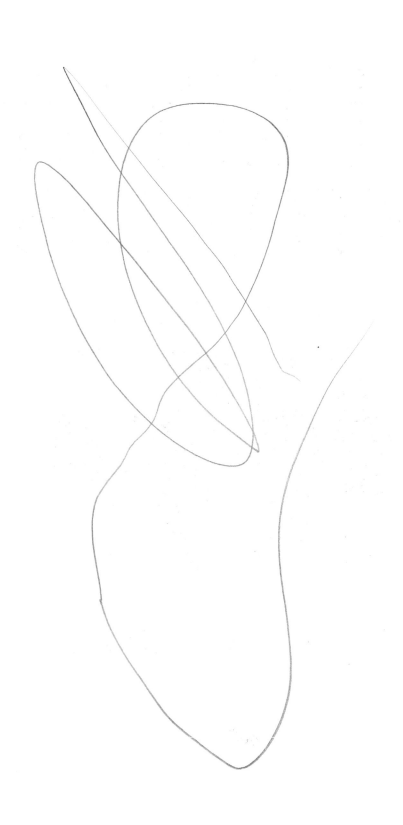

Contents

The Gingerbread Boy

There was once a little old man and a little old woman who had no children. One day the little old woman said, "I shall make myself a little boy out of gingerbread."

She mixed the dough, kneaded it well, and cut out and shaped a little gingerbread boy. She stuck on two raisins for eyes and three for buttons, and put a smile on his face. Then she popped him in the oven to bake.

When the little old woman opened the oven

door, out jumped the little gingerbread boy. He danced across the kitchen floor through the open door and ran off down the street. The little old man and the little old woman chased after him, shouting, "Stop, stop, little gingerbread boy!"

But the little gingerbread boy ran on ahead of them, calling:

> *"Run, run as fast as you can,*
> *You can't catch me,*
> *I'm the gingerbread man!"*

And the little old man and the little old woman couldn't catch him.

The little gingerbread boy ran on until he came to a cow in a meadow. "Stop, stop, little gingerbread boy!" said the cow. "You look good enough to eat."

But the little gingerbread boy ran past the cow, shouting, "I've run away from a little old man and a little old woman. I can run away from you too.

"Run, run, as fast as you can,
You can't catch me,
I'm the gingerbread man!"

And the cow couldn't catch him.

On and on ran the little gingerbread boy. He met a horse taking a drink at a stream.

"Hey, you, stop!" said the horse. "I want to see what you taste like."

But the little gingerbread boy skipped on past the horse, shouting, "I've run away from a little old man, a little old woman and a cow. I can run away from you too.

"Run, run, as fast as you can,
You can't catch me,
I'm the gingerbread man!"

And the horse couldn't catch him.

The little gingerbread boy ran faster and faster. He came to a farmer in a field.

"Stop, little gingerbread boy," cried the farmer. "I'll have you for my tea."

But the little gingerbread boy just darted between his legs, shouting, "I've run away from a little old man, a little old woman, a cow and a horse. I can run away from you too.

"Run, run, as fast as you can,
You can't catch me,
I'm the gingerbread man!"

The farmer chased him, but the little gingerbread boy was far too quick and the farmer couldn't catch him.

The little gingerbread boy ran on and on until he came to the big wide river. Then he stopped.

Just then a fox came trotting up. The fox thought the little gingerbread boy would make a tasty snack.

He was a clever, cunning fox, so he said, "I'll help you cross the river, little gingerbread boy. Sit on my tail and I'll swim you over to the other side."

And the little gingerbread boy climbed on to the fox's tail, and the fox began to swim across the river.

"You're getting wet," said the fox. "Why don't you jump on my back?"

So the little gingerbread boy jumped on to the fox's back.

When they were halfway across, the fox said, "You're too heavy to sit on my back. Why don't you jump on to my nose?"

So the little gingerbread boy jumped on to the fox's nose.

When they got to the other side the fox opened his jaws and went SNAP!

"Oh, dear me," said the little gingerbread boy, "I am half gone."

SNAP! went the fox a second time.

"Oh, dear me," said the little gingerbread boy. "I am three-quarters gone."

SNAP! went the fox a third time. And this time, there wasn't anything left at all of the little gingerbread boy.

The Three Little Pigs

Once upon a time there were three little pigs who went out into the world to seek their fortune.

The first little pig set off through the fields. There he met a man carrying a bundle of straw.

"Please, man," said the little pig, "will you give me some straw so that I can build myself a house?"

"As much as you need, little pig," said the man.

The man gave the straw to the little pig, and the little pig built himself a straw house.

In a little while a wolf came along and knocked on the door.

"Little pig, little pig," said the wolf, "let me come in."

"No, no, by the hair of my chinny, chin, chin, I will not let you in," said the little pig.

"Then I'll huff and I'll puff and I'll blow your house down," said the wolf.

And he huffed and he puffed and he blew the house down and ate up the little pig.

The second little pig went up the hill to the woods. There he met a man carrying a bundle of sticks.

"Please, man," said the little pig, "will you give me some sticks so that I can build myself a house?"

"As many as you need, little pig," said the man.

The man gave some sticks to the little pig, and

the little pig built himself a wooden house.

In a little while the wolf came along and knocked on the door.

"Little pig, little pig," said the wolf, "let me come in."

"No, no, by the hair of my chinny, chin, chin, I will not let you in," said the little pig.

"Then I'll huff and I'll puff and I'll blow your house down," snarled the wolf.

And he huffed and he puffed and he blew the house down and ate up the second little pig.

The third little pig skipped down the lane towards the town. On the way he met a man carrying a load of bricks.

"Please, man," said the little pig, "will you give me some bricks so that I can build myself a house?"

"As many as you need, little pig," said the man.

He gave some bricks to the little pig, and the little pig built himself a brick house.

No sooner had the little pig settled into his new home than the wolf came along and knocked at the door.

"Little pig, little pig," said the wolf, "let me come in."

"No, no, by the hair of my chinny, chin, chin, I will not let you in," said the little pig.

"Then I'll huff and I'll puff and I'll blow your house down," roared the wolf.

And he huffed and he puffed, and he huffed and he puffed, but he couldn't blow down the strong little brick house.

Then the wolf was angry. He sprang on to the roof and shouted, "Little pig, I'm coming down the chimney and I'm going to eat you up for my dinner!"

But the little pig was ready for the wolf. He

had a big pot of water boiling on the fire, and he lifted the lid and the wolf fell right into the pot. Then the little pig slammed the lid on again, and that was the end of the wicked wolf.

And the little pig lived safe and snug in his little brick house for the rest of his life.

Goldilocks
and the Three Bears

Once upon a time there were three bears who lived in a little cottage deep in the woods. There was a great big Father Bear, a middle-sized Mother Bear and a tiny wee Baby Bear.

Father Bear had a great big bowl to eat from, a great big chair to sit on, and a great big bed to sleep in. Mother Bear had a middle-sized bowl to eat from, a middle-sized chair to sit on, and a middle-sized bed to sleep in. And Baby Bear had a tiny wee bowl to eat from, a tiny wee chair to sit on, and a tiny wee bed to sleep in, all for himself.

One day, Mother Bear cooked the porridge for breakfast and ladled it into their three bowls; but the porridge was far too hot to eat. So the three bears went for a walk in the woods while they waited for it to cool.

The three bears had not been gone long when a little girl came by. She had wandered into the woods to pick flowers and was far from home. Her name was Goldilocks.

By now Goldilocks was tired and hungry, so she was pleased to see the three bears' cottage. She knocked on the door. There was no reply, but the door swung wide open and Goldilocks went inside!

She looked round the kitchen and saw the three bowls of porridge on the kitchen table where the bears had left them.

First she tasted the porridge in the great big bowl. "This porridge is too hot!" said Goldilocks.

Next she tasted the porridge in the medium-sized bowl. "This porridge is too cold!" said Goldilocks.

Then she tasted the porridge in the tiny wee bowl. "Mmm," she said, "this porridge is just right."

And she ate it all up.

Then she saw the bears' three chairs and thought she would sit down for a while.

First she sat on the great big chair, but that was too hard. Next she sat on the middle-sized chair, but that was too soft. Then she sat on the tiny wee chair, and that was just right. But all of a sudden the chair broke into pieces and down went Goldilocks on to the floor!

Then Goldilocks felt sleepy, so she went upstairs to the bedroom.

First she lay down on the great big bed, but it was too hard. Next she lay down on the middle-sized bed, but it was too soft. But when she lay down on the tiny wee bed it was just right and Goldilocks fell asleep at once.

While she was still sleeping the three bears came back from their walk in the woods. They went over to their bowls of porridge on the kitchen table.

"Who's been eating my porridge?" said Father Bear in his rough, gruff voice.

"Who's been eating my porridge?" said Mother Bear in her soft voice.

"Who's been eating my porridge? It's all gone!" said Baby Bear in his tiny wee voice.

Then the three bears looked at their chairs.

"Who's been sitting on my chair?" said Father Bear in his rough, gruff voice.

"Who's been sitting on my chair?" said Mother Bear in her soft voice.

"Who's been sitting on my chair and broken it all to bits?" said Baby Bear in his tiny wee voice and he started to cry.

Then the three bears went upstairs to their bedroom.

"Who's been sleeping in my bed?" said Father Bear in his rough, gruff voice.

"Who's been sleeping in my bed?" said Mother Bear in her soft voice.

"Who's sleeping in my bed? She's still there!" said Baby Bear in his tiny wee voice.

Goldilocks woke with a start. As soon as she saw the three bears, she jumped out of bed and ran down the stairs, out of the door, and away into the woods.

And that was the last the three bears ever saw of Goldilocks.

The Elves and the
Shoemaker

There was once a shoemaker who lived in a great city. He and his wife worked hard, but business was bad and they were so poor that one day they had nothing left to eat.

The shoemaker had only enough leather to make one pair of shoes, and no money to buy more. But he cut out the pieces of leather as carefully as he always did, and laid them on his workbench ready for the next day.

The next morning, when he went into his

workroom, the pieces of leather were gone. In their place was a pair of new shoes. They were beautifully made, with exquisite stitches so tiny and neat that you could not imagine who could have sewn them.

The shoemaker called his wife, and they were just admiring the shoes and wondering who had made them when a gentleman came into the shop.

"That's a fine pair of shoes," he said. "I'll have them." And he handed the shoemaker a golden coin.

So now the shoemaker had money to buy leather to make two more pairs of shoes, and there was enough to buy food as well.

That night the shoemaker cut out the pieces of leather and laid them on his workbench; and next morning there were two pairs of new shoes standing there. The shoes were so beautifully made that he sold them at once, and was able to buy more leather, and his wife got a chicken for their supper. Then the shoemaker cut out the pieces for another four pairs, and next morning a row of shoes stood on the workbench.

Every night the same thing happened, until the shoemaker and his wife were comfortably off.

"We must find out who is making these shoes," said the shoemaker one day.

So, instead of going to bed that night, they hid themselves in a corner of the workroom.

As the clock struck midnight, two little elves ran laughing and chattering into the room. They hadn't a stitch of clothing on. They scrambled up on to the workbench, picked up a piece of leather and set to work – so fast that the shoemaker and his wife could hardly see what was happening. Tap! tap! tap! went their tiny hammers, and their needles flashed as they sewed. Soon a whole row of shoes stood on the bench. Then the elves jumped down and ran away.

"Whatever can we do to thank them?" said the shoemaker.

"They must be cold without any clothes," said his wife. "I'll make them each a warm coat and a

pair of trousers, and knit them some woollen socks."

"And I'll make them some shoes from the very softest leather I can buy," said the shoemaker.

It took hours to cut out and sew such tiny things, but by the next night everything was ready. The shoemaker and his wife laid the clothes and shoes out neatly on the workbench. Then they hid in the corner and waited.

As the clock struck midnight, the elves came running in. They jumped up and down with excitement at the sight of the little coats and trousers, the woollen socks and soft leather shoes, and pulled them on and danced about the room.

Then they ran out of the door, and that was the last that was ever seen of them. But the shoe-maker always had work, and he and his wife lived happily for the rest of their lives.

The Cock, the Mouse and the Little Red Hen

Once upon a time there were three friends, a Cock, a Mouse and a Little Red Hen. They all lived together in a neat white house on a hill. The Little Red Hen did the cooking and cleaning, and kept everything as bright as a new pin.

At the bottom of the hill and across the stream there was a tumbledown house with peeling paint and dirty windows. A mother fox lived there with her four little foxes. They were always hungry.

One morning the mother fox said to her four little foxes, "I am going out to get some food. Put the pot on to boil, and lay the table ready for supper."

She picked up a dirty old sack, shut the door behind her and set off across the stream and up the hill to the neat white house where the Cock, the Mouse, and the Little Red Hen lived.

In the kitchen, the Little Red Hen was bustling about getting breakfast.

"Who'll fetch some sticks for the fire?" asked the Little Red Hen.

"I won't," said the Cock.

"I won't," said the Mouse.

"Then I'll fetch them myself," she said. And she ran and got the sticks and made a roaring fire.

"Who'll fetch some water from the spring?" asked the Little Red Hen.

"I won't," said the Cock.

"I won't," said the Mouse.

"Then I'll fetch it myself," she said. And she ran to the spring to fill the kettle.

The Little Red Hen made the breakfast and washed the dishes while the Cock and the Mouse sat and grumbled.

Then the Little Red Hen asked, "Who'll make the beds?"

"I won't," said the Cock.

"I won't," said the Mouse.

"Then I'll make them myself," said the Little Red Hen, and she bustled away up the stairs, while the Cock and the Mouse settled themselves in nice comfy armchairs to have a nap.

They were woken by a loud rat-tat-tat at the door.

"Who can that be? Little Red Hen should be here to answer the door," said the Mouse.

"Well, I'm not answering it. I'm too comfortable," said the Cock.

The Mouse opened the door and the Fox sprang inside.

"Cock-a-doodle-do!" crowed the Cock as he flew on to the back of the armchair.

"Oh, my! Oh, my!" squeaked the Mouse as she tried to run up the chimney.

But the Fox snatched the Mouse by the tail and pushed her into her sack, and she grabbed the Cock by the neck and stuffed him into the sack too.

Then the Little Red Hen came running downstairs to see what all the noise was about. As soon as the Fox saw her, she popped the Little Red Hen into the sack too.

Then she tied the sack tightly, threw it over her shoulder and set off down the hill. Poor

Cock! Poor Mouse! Poor Little Red Hen!

"I wish I hadn't been so cross," said the Cock.

"I wish I hadn't been so lazy," said the Mouse.

"Never mind, I'll think of something," said the Little Red Hen.

By this time the Fox was feeling tired. Her load was heavy and it was a hot day. So she dumped the sack on the ground, lay down under a tree, and fell fast asleep.

"Now we can get out!" whispered the Little Red Hen when she heard the Fox's snore.

She took a little pair of scissors out of her apron pocket and snipped a hole in the sacking. The Cock, the Mouse and the Little Red Hen scrambled out through the hole.

"Now we must find three stones to put in the sack," said the Little Red Hen.

And they did. They rolled three heavy stones up to the sack and pushed them inside through the hole. Then the Little Red Hen got her needle and thread out of her apron pocket and sewed up the hole.

The Cock, the Mouse and the Little Red Hen ran all the way home to their neat white house as fast as their legs would carry them. They slammed and locked the door and closed all the shutters and then they felt safe again.

The Fox woke up just as the sun was setting. She slung the sack over her shoulder and set off again.

"This sack feels heavier than ever. The four

little foxes will have a wonderful supper tonight," said the Fox.

But, as she took the first step across the stream, she sank up to her waist. She took a second step, and sank right to the bottom. So the four little foxes didn't get their supper that night after all.

As for the Cock and the Mouse, they were never lazy or bad-tempered again. The Little Red Hen enjoyed a well-earned rest while the Cock and the Mouse did all the work, and they all lived happily together for the rest of their lives.

The Musicians of Bremen

Once upon a time there was a donkey who worked hard for his master all his life, carrying sacks of corn to the mill.

One day the donkey's master said to him, "I'll have to get rid of you. You're too old and slow to be useful any more."

This made the donkey very unhappy. Then he said to himself, "I can still bray beautifully. The other donkeys often say what a fine voice I have. I shall go to Bremen and sing with the town band."

So he trot-trotted down the road to Bremen.

He had not gone very far before he met a dog. The dog was lying by the roadside, barking.

"Why are you barking like that?" asked the donkey.

"My master has thrown me out," said the dog. "He says I'm too old to herd the sheep any more."

"Why don't you come to Bremen with me?" said the donkey. "You can bark and I can bray and together we can join the town band."

"I'd like that," said the dog, and he wagged his tail.

So the donkey trot-trotted and the dog patter-patted along the road to Bremen.

Before long they met a cat sitting on a wall, miaowing.

"Why are you miaowing like that?" asked the donkey.

"My mistress has sent me away," said the cat. "She says I'm too old to catch mice."

"Why don't you come to Bremen with us?" said the donkey. "You can miaow, the dog can bark, I can bray, and together we can join the town band."

"I'd like that," said the cat.

So the donkey trot-trotted, the dog patter-patted and the cat pad-padded along the road to Bremen.

After a while they came to a farm where a cockerel was sitting on a gatepost. He was crowing with all his might.

"Why are you crowing so loudly?" asked the donkey.

"The farmer's wife says I'm too old to be useful any more," said the cockerel. "So I'm making as much noise as I can before she puts me in the pot."

"Why don't you come to Bremen with us?" said the donkey. "You can crow, the cat can miaow, the dog can bark, and I can bray, and together we can join the town band."

The cockerel let out a loud cock-a-doodle-doo! and flew down to join them.

So the donkey trot-trotted, the dog patter-patted, the cat pad-padded and the cockerel scritch-scratched along the road to Bremen.

They were halfway to the town when it began to grow dark. So they stopped at a farmhouse to see if they could get some food and a place to sleep.

The donkey went up to the house and peered in through a window. He could see a band of fierce robbers sitting round a table piled high with things to eat.

The donkey and his friends were hungry.

They wanted some of the food. So they thought of a clever way to outwit the robbers.

First of all the donkey put his hooves on the window sill. The dog scrambled up on his back. The cat climbed on to the dog's shoulder. And the cockerel flew up and perched on the cat's head.

Then they all started singing together at the tops of their voices. The donkey brayed, the dog barked, the cat miaowed and the cockerel crowed.

What a terrible noise they made! The robbers were so scared they jumped up from the table and ran out of the house as fast as their legs would carry them.

The four friends went inside and ate up all the food. Then they put out the candles and settled down to sleep. The donkey lay down outside the house, the dog stretched out behind the door, the cat curled up beside the fire and the cockerel roosted on a rafter.

While they were asleep one of the robbers

came back to the house, opened the door and crept inside.

First he trod on the cat, who hissed and spat and scratched his arm.

"Ouch!" yowled the robber and he stumbled back to the door.

Then he tripped over the dog, who jumped up and bit him on the leg.

"Aargh!" yowled the robber and he staggered out into the farmyard.

Then he bumped into the donkey, who gave him a sharp kick.

"Eeek!" shrieked the robber as he reached the farm gate.

There the cockerel flew at him, flapping his wings in the robber's face and screeching in his ears.

And the fierce robber ran back into the forest, and was never seen again.

So the donkey, the dog, the cat and the cockerel were left in peace. The farmhouse suited them so well that they stayed there and lived happily together. And they never did go and sing with the Bremen town band.

Country Mouse and
Town Mouse

There was once a country mouse who lived in a little house under the hedgerow. Every day he swept his house clean and went out into the fields to find seeds and nuts and fruits for his larder. He worked hard, but he was happy for he had everything he needed.

One day Country Mouse's cousin from the town came to stay. Country Mouse was so pleased to see Town Mouse that he made her a bed of sweet-smelling hay and gathered the plumpest nuts, grains and berries he could find for her to eat.

But at suppertime Town Mouse said, "Dear cousin, is this all you eat? You should come and visit me in the town. I live in a fine big house where there is as much food as you want. I just help myself whenever I'm hungry."

After supper Country Mouse showed Town Mouse the bed he had prepared for her.

"Do you really expect me to spend the night on that bundle of hay?" said Town Mouse. "I shan't sleep a wink. I have a soft feather bed at home; you should come and try it."

Town Mouse curled up on the hay and fell fast asleep. But Country Mouse couldn't sleep for a long time. He kept thinking about the fine big house his cousin lived in, and her soft feather bed.

Next day Country Mouse took Town Mouse to the cornfield. But Town Mouse complained that the corn stalks scratched her; and when a weasel

came by and the two mice had to crouch down and hide, she was terrified out of her wits.

"What a horrible creature!" said Town Mouse. "I don't know how you can stand it here."

Country Mouse took Town Mouse back to his house and gave her a delicious supper of berries. But Town Mouse said, "I really don't think I like the country. I shall go home tomorrow. Why don't you come and stay with me? Then you'll see how much pleasanter it is to live in the town."

"Oh yes, please, I'd love to come," said

Country Mouse. And the next day he locked up his little house and the two mice set off for the town.

It was getting dark when they arrived and Country Mouse's eyes were dazzled by the bright lights. Town Mouse scurried on in front and Country Mouse tried to keep close to her, but he was frightened by the lights and the heavy tramp of people's feet as they walked past.

At last they came to Town Mouse's house. It was just as big and fine as she had described.

"This way," said Town Mouse, disappearing into a hole in the wall.

So Country Mouse followed her, down a long dark passage and through another hole into the kitchen.

Country Mouse began to feel better at once, for there, laid out on a table, were all kinds of wonderful things to eat; bread and butter, fruit cake, a wedge of cheese, a bowl of strawberries and a jug of cream.

"Come on, you can eat as much as you like," said Town Mouse.

Country Mouse climbed on to the table, trembling with excitement.

He had just started nibbling at the cheese when the door burst open and in came the cook. Country Mouse scuttled behind the strawberries and crouched down, quivering with fear.

When the cook had left the kitchen, Country Mouse looked around for his cousin but couldn't see her anywhere. What he did see was an enormous cat, sitting by the fire.

Country Mouse was terrified and didn't know what to do. Oh, where was Town Mouse?

Country Mouse began to think he would never see his little house under the hedgerow again.

Then he heard Town Mouse call out in a loud whisper. "Over here, cousin. Make a run for it!"

Country Mouse climbed down from the table and shot across the floor to Town Mouse. Together they squeezed through the nearest hole in the floorboards.

Country Mouse was trembling all over, but Town Mouse just laughed. "Don't worry," she said, "I'll make sure you get a good meal tomorrow."

That night Country Mouse curled up on Town Mouse's feather bed. He lay awake all night, listening to the cat mewing outside the mousehole.

Next day Country Mouse said to Town Mouse, "It was very kind of you to show me your home, but I really must be going."

"You can't leave before you have a proper meal," said Town Mouse. "Besides, there's so much to see in the town."

"I think I've seen enough, thank you," said Country Mouse.

And with a quick goodbye, he scampered back to the hole in the wall and ran through the town and all the way home.

And from that day onwards he stayed in his little house under the hedgerow, and never dreamed of living in the town again.

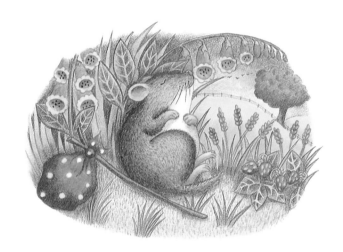

The Three Billy Goats Gruff

Once upon a time there were three billy goats called Big Billy Goat Gruff, Little Billy Goat Gruff and Baby Billy Goat Gruff.

They lived on a rocky hillside where they had only dry grass and thistles to eat. On the hill on the other side of the valley the grass was lush and juicy, and the three billy goats longed to taste it.

But to get to the other side of the valley the billy goats had to cross a bridge over the stream.

Underneath this bridge lived a great ugly troll, and the billy goats were frightened of him.

One day Baby Billy Goat Gruff said, "I'm hungry!"

Little Billy Goat Gruff said, "I'm hungry too. If only we could get to that luscious grass on the other side of the valley!"

And Big Billy Goat Gruff said, "We must find a way to cross the bridge safely. I will think of a plan." And he did.

Next day Baby Billy Goat Gruff trotted down to the stream. Trip, trap, trip, trap, went his hooves on the bridge.

"Who's that?" bellowed the troll.

"It's only me," said Baby Billy Goat Gruff.

"I'll gobble you up if you cross the bridge," said the troll.

"Please don't. I'm so small that I won't be good to eat," said Baby Billy Goat Gruff. He was trying to be brave but really his legs were trembling. "Why don't you wait until my big brother comes along? He's plumper than I am."

"Oh, all right then," said the troll. "Be off with you."

So Baby Billy Goat Gruff crossed the bridge and ran up the hillside to eat the juicy grass.

Then Little Billy Goat Gruff came down to the stream. Trip, trap, trip, trap, went his hooves on the bridge.

"Who's that?" bellowed the troll.

"It's only me!" said Little Billy Goat Gruff.

"I'll gobble you up if you cross the bridge," said the troll.

"Please don't. I'm not very big, and I won't be good to eat," said Little Billy Goat Gruff with a shiver of fright. "Why don't you wait until my big brother comes along? He'll be nice and tasty."

"Oh, all right then," said the troll. "Be off with you."

So Little Billy Goat Gruff crossed the bridge and ran up the hillside to join his baby brother.

Then along came Big Billy Goat Gruff. Now he really was *very* big, with strong sturdy legs and long curving horns.

When *he* crossed the bridge it creaked and groaned at every step.

"Who's that who dares to cross my bridge?" roared the troll.

"It's me!" said Big Billy Goat Gruff.

"Then I'm coming to gobble you up," said the troll, and he sprang out on to the bridge.

What a horrible fearsome-looking creature he was! But Big Billy Goat Gruff wasn't a bit afraid.

"Oh, you are, are you," he said. "We'll just see about that."

And putting his head down low, he charged at the troll and butted him hard. SPLASH! went the troll as he fell into the stream, and that was the end of him.

So Big Billy Goat Gruff went trip, trap, trip, trap across the bridge and ran up the hillside to join his brothers. And they have lived there from that day to this, enjoying the lush, juicy grass.

Teeny-Tiny

Once upon a time there was a teeny-tiny woman who lived in a teeny-tiny house in a teeny-tiny village.

One day she put on her bonnet and went out for a walk. And when the teeny-tiny woman had gone a teeny-tiny way, she came to a teeny-tiny gate. She opened the teeny-tiny gate and went into a teeny-tiny churchyard.

And when the teeny-tiny woman had got into the teeny-tiny churchyard, she saw a teeny-tiny

59

bone on a teeny-tiny grave. And the teeny-tiny woman said, "This teeny-tiny bone will make a teeny-tiny bowl of soup for my supper."

So the teeny-tiny woman put the teeny-tiny bone into her teeny-tiny pocket, and went back to her teeny-tiny house.

Now, when she got home, she was a bit tired. So she went upstairs to her teeny-tiny bed and put the teeny-tiny bone into a teeny-tiny cupboard.

Then the teeny-tiny woman got into bed, and went to sleep. She was woken by a teeny-tiny voice from the teeny-tiny cupboard, which said:

"Give me my bone!"

The teeny-tiny woman was a teeny-tiny bit frightened, so she hid her head under the bedclothes and went to sleep again.

Then the teeny-tiny voice cried out a teeny-tiny bit louder:

"Give me my bone!"

This made the teeny-tiny woman a teeny-tiny bit more frightened, so she hid her head a teeny-tiny bit further under the bedclothes.

Then the teeny-tiny voice cried out again a teeny-tiny bit louder still, and it said:

"Give me my bone!"

And this time the teeny-tiny woman put her head out from under the bedclothes and said in her loudest voice:

"TAKE IT!"

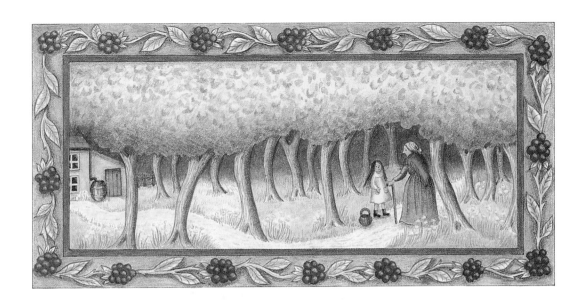

The Little Porridge Pot

There was once a little girl who lived with her mother in a little house on the edge of a village. They were very poor and the day came when they had nothing left to eat.

So the mother sent the little girl out into the forest to pick berries. She hadn't gone very far when she met an old woman.

"You look hungry, little girl," said the old woman.

"Oh, I am," said the little girl. "My mother and

I have no food left at home and no money to buy any."

"I can help you," said the old woman, and she took a little cooking pot from her bag. "Take this pot, my dear. And when you say to it, 'Cook, little pot, cook,' it will hiss and bubble and fill with steaming hot porridge. And when you have enough, you can say, 'Stop, little pot, stop'. Then it will stop cooking."

"Oh, thank you," said the little girl and she ran all the way home to her mother. Her mother put the pot on the stove right away.

"Cook, little pot, cook," said the little girl. And at once the pot began to hiss and bubble and to fill with steaming hot porridge.

The little girl and her mother sat down and ate and ate until they could eat no more. Then the little girl said, "Stop, little pot, stop," and the pot stopped cooking.

The little girl and her mother danced round the table for joy for they knew they would never go hungry again.

One day, when the little girl was away visiting her grandmother, her mother got out the little pot and set it on the table to make some lunch.

"Cook, little pot, cook," said the little girl's mother. And at once the pot began to hiss and bubble and fill with porridge.

The little girl's mother helped herself and ate until she was full. Then she said, "Enough, little pot." But the pot went right on cooking. The porridge bubbled out of the pot, over the table and on to the floor.

"Oh dear, oh dear! Whatever shall I do?" wailed the little girl's mother. Try as she would, she just couldn't remember how to stop the pot cooking.

By now the porridge was pouring out through the door into the garden. And it didn't stop there! It streamed into the house next door and along the street into all the neighbours' houses! Before long the whole village was full of porridge, and all the villagers had run away.

Just then the little girl came home from her grandmother's. "Stop, little pot, stop," she said and the little pot stopped cooking.

And all the villagers had to eat their way back home again.

The Turnip

There was once a little old man who worked all year round growing vegetables to feed himself and his wife.

One spring day he planted some turnip seeds, all in a row. He covered them over with soil and watered them well.

"Grow, little seeds, grow," he said.

And they did. Soon tiny green shoots peeped up through the soil and the plants grew strong and sturdy.

But one turnip grew much faster than all the rest. It grew and grew. First it was twice the size of the others, then four times bigger, then eight times bigger, and it just went on growing.

One day the little old man's wife said to him, "Why don't you pull up that enormous turnip, so we can have nice turnip stew for supper tonight?"

So the little old man went out into the garden, took a firm grasp of the enormous turnip and

pulled. But the turnip didn't budge, no, not one bit.

So the little old man shouted to his wife.

The little old woman pulled the little old man, and the little old man pulled the turnip. But still the turnip didn't budge, no, not one bit.

So the little old woman went next door to fetch the little girl who lived there.

The little girl pulled the little old woman, the little old woman pulled the little old man, and the little old man pulled the turnip. But still the turnip didn't budge, no, not one bit.

So the little girl ran to fetch her brother.

And the little boy pulled the little girl, the little girl pulled the little old woman, the little old woman pulled the little old man, and the little old man pulled the turnip. But still the turnip didn't budge, no, not one bit.

So the little boy whistled for his dog.

The dog pulled the little boy, the little boy pulled the little girl, the little girl pulled the little old woman, the little old woman pulled the little

old man, and the little old man pulled the turnip. But still the turnip didn't budge, no, not one bit.

So the dog barked for the cat.

The cat pulled the dog, the dog pulled the little boy, the little boy pulled the little girl, the little girl pulled the little old woman, the little old woman pulled the little old man, and the little old man pulled the turnip. But still the turnip didn't budge, no, not one bit.

So the cat mewed for the mouse.

And the mouse pulled the cat, the cat pulled the dog, the dog pulled the little boy, the little

boy pulled the little girl, the little girl pulled the little old woman, the little old woman pulled the little old man, and the little old man pulled the turnip.

The earth cracked, the ground gave way and out came the enormous turnip . . . at last!

The little old woman cooked an enormous turnip stew for supper, and the mouse, the cat, the dog, the little boy, the little girl, the little old woman and the little old man all sat down together to eat it. And it was the tastiest meal they ever had in their lives.

The Hedgehog and
the Hare

There was once a hedgehog who lived with his wife near a field of cabbages and turnips.

One summer morning, Hedgehog decided to go for a walk to see how his turnips were doing.

He trundled up the path to the turnip field, where he was surprised to see a hare nibbling at his cabbages. But Hare thought the field belonged to him and that the cabbages were *his*.

Hedgehog was a friendly creature and said,

"Good morning, Hare. What a lovely day."

But Hare took not the slightest notice. He just went on eating.

"I thought I'd have a walk before breakfast, to see how my turnips are doing," said Hedgehog.

"A walk before breakfast!" said Hare scornfully. "You won't get far with those short legs."

Hedgehog was hurt by this. He knew his legs were short but they always took him wherever he wanted to go. So he said, "You can be unkind about my legs if you like, but I bet if we ran a race I'd win it."

"You, run faster than me! No one runs faster

than I do," said Hare. "I tell you what – we'll have a race. And then we'll see how well you can run. And if you beat me, you can have my golden coin and my flask of brandy."

"All right," said Hedgehog. "But I must go home for my breakfast first. I'll meet you at the far end of the field in half an hour."

Now Hedgehog was sharper-witted than Hare. He had already thought of a way of winning the race.

He went home and told his wife his plan. "You must hide at the finishing post and pop up when you see Hare coming. He will think that you are me and that I have won the race. And won't he be angry!"

Hedgehog set off back for the field where Hare was already waiting for him, eager to start.

"Right, I'm ready," said Hedgehog. "You run along one furrow and I'll keep to another."

So Hare and Hedgehog lined up. Hare shouted, "Ready! Steady! Go!" and Hare shot away, running like the wind. Hedgehog started running too, as fast as his legs would carry him.

When Hare reached the finishing post at the far end of the field, he heard a voice saying, "Ya-hoo, Hare. I've beaten you," and up popped Mrs Hedgehog's head out of a furrow. But of course Hare thought it was Hedgehog.

"How did you do it? It must be a mistake!" said Hare. "We must run the race again."

So Hare and Hedgehog went back to the starting line and ran the race again. And again as Hare reached the finishing line, up popped Mrs Hedgehog's head.

"Ya-hoo," she said. "I've beaten you again."

"You can't possibly run faster than I do. Let's try again."

So they did. They ran again, and again, and again, but each time the same thing happened.

At last Hare fell down exhausted. "All right, you win," he said, gasping for breath. "But I don't know how you did it. I suppose I'll have to give you the flask of brandy and golden coin that I promised you."

Hedgehog was delighted that he had outwitted Hare and he tucked the golden coin and the flask of brandy under his arm and set off home with his wife to enjoy a good meal.

The Ugly Duckling

Once upon a time there was a mother duck who lived beside a lake with her nine ducklings. Eight of them were pretty fluffy little yellow ducklings but the ninth one was a dirty grey colour, with a long thin neck.

"What an ugly little duckling you are!" his mother would say to him. And his brothers and sisters would tease him and peck him and try to chase him away.

"You don't belong in our family, you're too

ugly!" they would say. "Go away! We don't want you here."

So the ugly duckling kept away from his brothers and sisters. When their mother took her ducklings for a walk along the shore of the lake, or taught them to swim and dive under the water to catch insects, he always lagged behind. He was very unhappy.

When the ducklings could swim well enough, their mother took them to visit the ducks who lived on the other side of the lake.

She set off across the water with the nine little ducklings paddling behind her in a long line. As usual the ugly duckling was at the very back and was the last to waddle out of the water.

As soon as the other ducks saw him, they started picking on him.

"What's this ugly creature?" said one of the drakes, giving him a sharp poke.

"You can't possibly be a duck," said another.

"I am a duck! I am!" cried the ugly duckling. And he ran away and hid in some reeds, so that none of the other ducks could laugh at him.

Soon it grew dark. The ugly duckling wanted his mother, but he couldn't see where she had

gone. He wandered about on the side of the lake, unable to find his way home. Feeling very small and lonely, he curled up and went to sleep. How he wished he was back home with his mother, even if all the others did make fun of him!

The next morning, as the ugly duckling dabbled around in the water looking for food, two wild ducks flew up.

"What kind of bird are you?" asked one.

"I'm a duck," said the ugly duckling.

"Funny kind of duck!" said one wild duck to the other.

So the ugly duckling ran away from the wild ducks, stumbling across marshes, over fields, through meadows, until he came to another lake.

"I'll stay here," he said. "There are some reeds to hide in and there'll be plenty of food."

The ugly duckling stayed there all through the winter. It was cold, and an icy wind blew from the north.

One day he saw some swans flying south. The ugly duckling gazed up at them longingly. They were so beautiful, with their great white wings beating slowly through the sky.

"Why don't you come with us?" they called down to him.

"Wait for me! I'm coming!" he cried.

He flapped his wings and tried to take off, but he couldn't fly very well, and the big white swans were soon far away.

The winter was long but one day the ugly duckling felt the sun warm on his back again. He stretched out his wings. They were big and very strong now and he took off into the air with ease.

"I'm flying! I'm really flying!" cried the ugly duckling.

He flew on till he came to a broad river. There he saw some swans gliding along, their long necks proudly arched. The ugly duckling landed on the river bank.

"Come and join us," said the swans.

"Who, me?" asked the ugly duckling. "You don't want me! I'm only an ugly duckling."

"A duckling? Why, you're a swan just like us. Look at yourself," said one of the swans.

The ugly duckling looked down into the water. It was not an ugly duckling he saw there at all, but a beautiful white swan just like the others. He was no longer a clumsy duckling but as graceful as they were. The other swans gathered around him and together they swam off downstream. And the ugly duckling who had become a swan lived happily ever after.

Henny-Penny

One day Henny-Penny was walking in the farmyard when all of a sudden an acorn fell and hit her on the head.

"Goodness gracious," said Henny-Penny. "The sky is falling. I must go and tell the king."

She hurried along until she met Cocky-Locky.

"Where are you going, Henny-Penny?" asked Cocky-Locky.

"I'm going to tell the king the sky is falling," said Henny-Penny.

"Then I'll come with you," said Cocky-Locky.

So Henny-Penny and Cocky-Locky went to tell the king the sky was falling. They hurried along until they met Ducky-Lucky.

"Where are you going, Henny-Penny and Cocky-Locky?" asked Ducky-Lucky.

"We're going to tell the king the sky is falling," said Henny-Penny and Cocky-Locky.

"Then I'll come with you," said Ducky-Lucky.

So Henny-Penny, Cocky-Locky and Ducky-Lucky went to tell the king the sky was falling. They hurried along until they met Goosey-Poosey.

"Where are you going, Henny-Penny, Cocky-Locky and Ducky-Lucky?" asked Goosey-Poosey.

"We're going to tell the king the sky is falling," said Henny-Penny, Cocky-Locky and Ducky-Lucky.

"Then I'll come with you," said Goosey-Poosey.

So Henny-Penny, Cocky-Locky, Ducky-

Lucky and Goosey-Poosey went to tell the king the sky was falling. They hurried along until they met Turkey-Lurkey.

"Where are you going, Henny-Penny, Cocky-Locky, Ducky-Lucky and Goosey-Poosey?" asked Turkey-Lurkey.

"We're going to tell the king the sky is falling," said Henny-Penny, Cocky-Locky, Ducky-Lucky and Goosey-Poosey.

"Then I'll come with you," said Turkey-Lurkey.

So Henny-Penny, Cocky-Locky, Ducky-Lucky, Goosey-Poosey and Turkey-Lurkey went to tell the king the sky was falling. They hurried along until they met Foxy-Loxy.

"Where are you going, Henny-Penny, Cocky-Locky, Ducky-Lucky, Goosey-Poosey and Turkey-Lurkey?" asked Foxy-Loxy.

"We're going to tell the king the sky is falling," said Henny-Penny, Cocky-Locky, Ducky-Lucky, Goosey-Poosey and Turkey-Lurkey.

"Oh, but you're not going the right way to the

king," said Foxy-Loxy. "Shall I show you the best path to take?"

"Yes, please," they all said.

So Henny-Penny, Cocky-Locky, Ducky-Lucky, Goosey-Poosey, Turkey-Lurkey and Foxy-Loxy went to tell the king the sky was falling. They hurried along until they came to a dark hole.

Now this was really the entrance to Foxy-Loxy's den. But Foxy-Loxy said, "This is the quickest way to the king. Follow me."

Foxy-Loxy went into his den and Turkey-Lurkey followed him. They hadn't gone very far when all of a sudden Foxy-Loxy turned round and CRUNCH! he ate up Turkey-Lurkey in one great gulp. Then CRUNCH! he ate up Goosey-Poosey and CRUNCH! he ate up Ducky-Lucky too.

Foxy-Loxy was just about to take a big bite of Cocky-Locky when Cocky-Locky called out, "Cock-a-doodle-doo! Henny-Penny, run for your life!"

Then CRUNCH! Cocky-Locky was eaten up too.

And Henny-Penny ran all the way home to the farmyard and never did tell the king the sky was falling.

Little Red Riding Hood

Once upon a time there was a little girl who lived with her mother in a little house on the edge of the woods. She was a kind little girl and everyone loved her. She was known as Little Red Riding Hood because she always wore a red cloak with a hood which her grandmother had made for her.

One day Little Red Riding Hood's mother said to her, "Your grandmother is not very well and I want you to go and see her. Take her this basket of eggs and this pot of honey. Go straight to your grandmother's cottage and don't wander off the path. And whatever you do, don't speak to any strangers on the way."

Little Red Riding Hood promised to do as she was told. She kissed her mother goodbye, took her basket and set off. As she turned to take the path through the trees, she saw a woodcutter and gave him a friendly wave.

Little Red Riding Hood had not gone far into the woods when she met a wolf.

"Good morning, little girl," said the wolf with a wicked smile. He was thinking what a sweet-tasting meal she would make. "Where are you going?" he said.

"I'm going to see my grandmother," said Little Red Riding Hood. "She's not at all well, so I'm taking her this basket of eggs and this pot of honey."

"Why don't you take her some flowers too?" said the wolf.

"What a good idea," said Little Red Riding Hood, putting down her basket. She had quite forgotten what her mother had told her. And she left the path to pick some wild flowers.

The wolf ran off and went straight to her grandmother's cottage. He knocked on the door.

"Who's there?" called out Little Red Riding Hood's grandmother.

"It's only me, Little Red Riding Hood," said the wolf in a high voice.

"Then lift the latch and come in, my dear," said Little Red Riding Hood's grandmother.

The wolf threw open the door and sprang into the room. He gobbled up Little Red Riding Hood's grandmother in one great gulp. Then he put on her nightgown and nightcap and jumped into bed. Pulling the quilt right up to his nose, he waited for Little Red Riding Hood to arrive.

Before long Little Red Riding Hood came walking up the path carrying her basket and an armful of flowers.

She knocked gently at the door. "Who's

there?" said the wolf in a frail voice like Little Red Riding Hood's grandmother.

"It's only me, Grandmother," said Little Red Riding Hood. "I've brought you some flowers and some good things to eat."

"Then lift the latch and come in, my dear," said the wolf.

Little Red Riding Hood lifted the latch and went in.

She put down her basket and flowers on the

bedside table. Then she looked at the wolf lying in her grandmother's bed.

"Oh, Grandmother, what big eyes you have," said Little Red Riding Hood.

"All the better to see you with, my dear," said the wolf.

"Oh, Grandmother, what big ears you have," said Little Red Riding Hood.

"All the better to hear you with, my dear," said the wolf.

"Oh, Grandmother, what big teeth you have," said Little Red Riding Hood.

"All the better to EAT you with, my dear," said the wolf, and he leapt out of bed and gobbled up Little Red Riding Hood. Then he lay down again and fell sound asleep.

The woodcutter who was passing the cottage heard the wolf's snores and went in to see what had happened. As soon as he saw the wolf he lifted his axe and with one mighty blow across the stomach killed the wicked wolf dead. To his surprise, out scrambled Little Red Riding Hood and her grandmother, safe and sound.

Then Little Red Riding Hood gave her grandmother the eggs and the pot of honey, and put the flowers in a vase. And they all sat down to have some tea.

And from that day onwards Little Red Riding Hood never strayed from the path again and she never stopped to speak to strangers.

Daniel Libeskind

J8